Belinda
in
PARIS

by Amy Young

viking

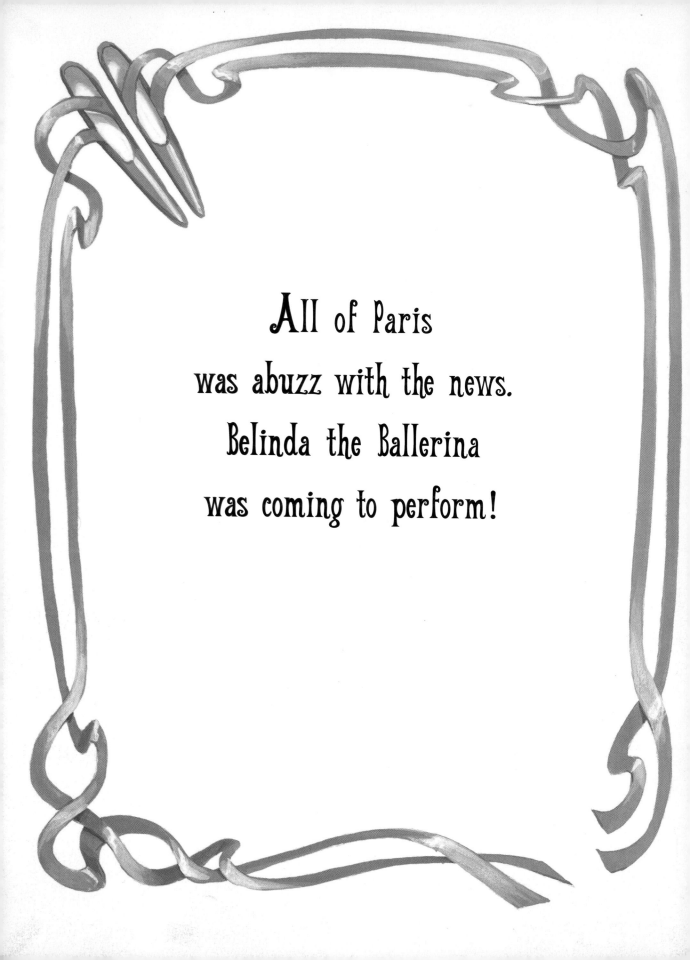

All of Paris
was abuzz with the news.
Belinda the Ballerina
was coming to perform!

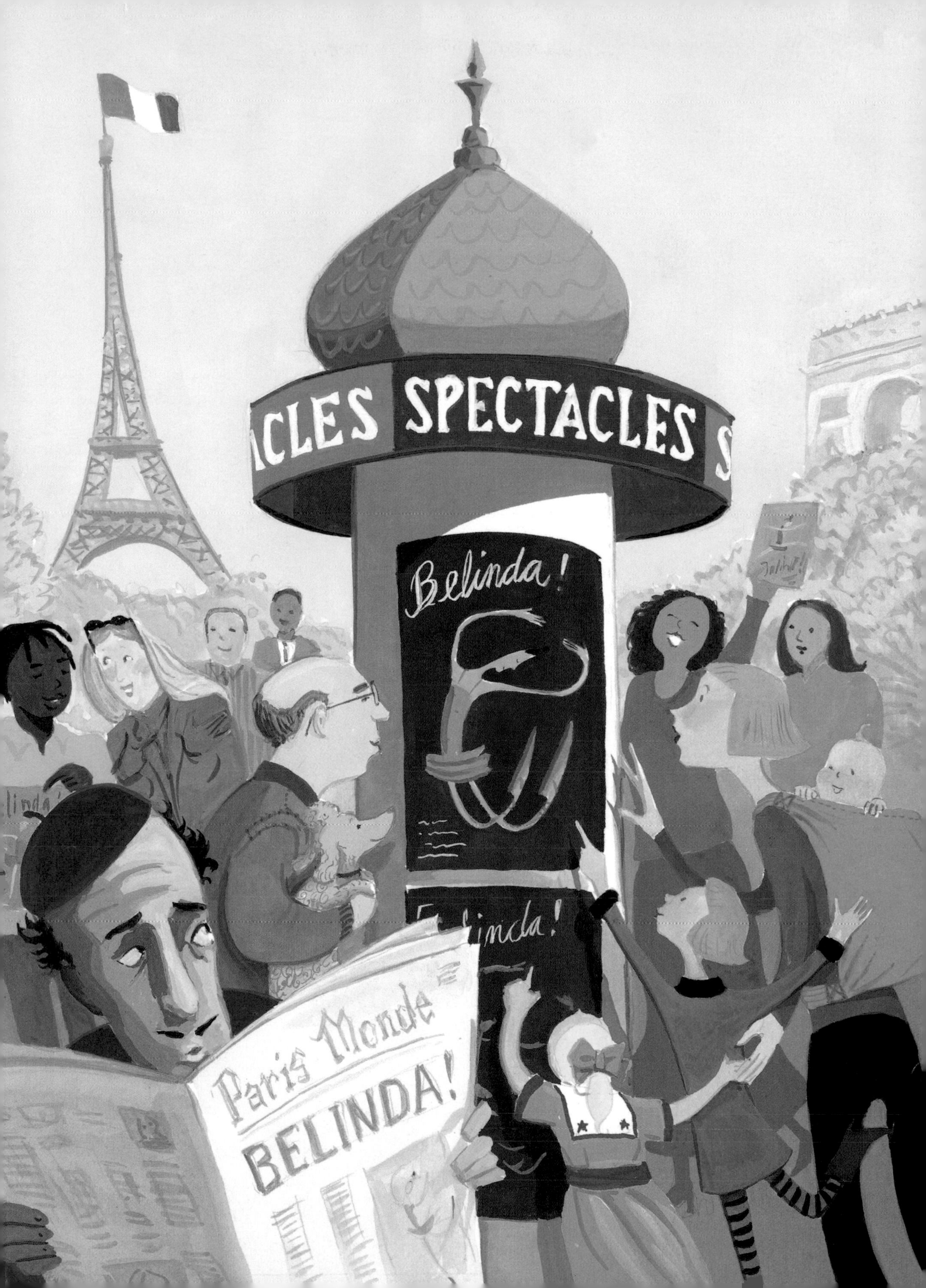
ACLES SPECTACLES S
Belinda!
Belinda!
Paris Monde
BELINDA!
BELINDA

"Belinda is coming!" said the
grocer to the lady in pink.

"Belinda is coming!"
said the lady in pink
to her friend.

"Belinda is coming!"
said the friend to
everyone she knew.

CAFÉ L'OISEAU

Only one person in the whole city was not
looking forward to Belinda's performance.

That was Belinda.

It was not that her tutu was
a little too tight, which it was.

It was not that this was a very
important performance with the
best ballet company in Paris, which it was.

No. It was that when Belinda got to Paris, she was told,
"Ah, Mademoiselle, we regret that your shoes went to Pago
Pago. But do not worry, you will have them in a week."

Belinda *was* worried. Her performance was that night.
Without the right shoes, she would be a flop!

Belinda went to the ballet company and broke the bad news. "You need new pointe shoes!" said the littlest ballerina, Gabrielle. "Let's go!"

Gabrielle led Belinda through the streets of Paris

to a store that sold ballet shoes.

"Ooh la la!" said the clerk when he saw the size of Belinda's feet. He brought out the biggest shoes in the store . . .

but they didn't quite fit.

"There is not a shoe in all of Paris that will fit such magnificent feet," he said. "You must have them specially made. Try Monsieur Luc, the cobbler."

Gabrielle and Belinda hurried off
to find Monsieur Luc.

When Monsieur Luc saw Belinda's feet he threw up his hands.
"I do not have enough fabric! I do not have a form so grand!

"Bring me those things and I can help you. But I must tell
you, I have never seen such a form. As to fabric, Madame
Sophia's is the best, but who knows if she will have enough?"

Belinda and Gabrielle decided to
look for the fabric first. They set
off to find Madame Sophia.

As they passed a bakery, they noticed a man with a big
platter of food. It was Monsieur Fromage, the baker.
"Have some quiche!" he said. "A croissant? An éclair?"

"Thank you, but we are in a hurry," said Belinda.
"What a shame!" said Monsieur Fromage sadly. "A big party
was just canceled. All this beautiful food will go to waste."

When Belinda and Gabrielle reached Madame Sophia's,
they found the shop in an uproar.

"Madame," said Gabrielle, "this is Belinda the—"

"Not now!" cried Madame Sophia. "I have a fashion
gala in one hour and my caterer just had an accident.
The party is ruined!"

Le Party
CATERER

"Maybe not," said Belinda. "What if we helped get food for your party?"
"I would do anything!" wept Madame Sophia.

In no time at all it was arranged. Monsieur Fromage was ecstatic.

Madame Sophia was so happy that she gave Belinda
a huge piece of pink silk.

"But we still need a form," said Gabrielle. "And the performance is only a few hours away!"
Belinda thought hard. Suddenly she had an idea.

She asked Monsieur Fromage for a favor—two favors, really—and then she and Gabrielle hurried back to the cobbler's shop.

"*Voilà!*" Monsieur Luc cried.

"Beautiful silk for the shoe . . .

"... and beautiful baguettes for the form!
You are a clever girl!"

Belinda stretched and limbered up while Monsieur Luc

measured

and cut

and stitched

and tucked.

The new shoes were *perfect*!

That night, everyone in Paris agreed they had never seen such marvelous dancing.

"It is the baguettes, which are just
the right size and shape," said
Monsieur Fromage, beaming.

"It is the pink silk, which glistens and shines,"
said Madame Sophia, smiling.

"It is my fine workmanship, which
has given her a most excellent shoe,"
boasted the cobbler.

"It is all of that," Gabrielle said,

"but most of all, it is Belinda. She is *magnifique*."

Dedicated to Ann and Bob Cooper and to Gabrielle Thiam
(the *real* Gabrielle), with love and thanks.

WITH GRATEFUL ACKNOWLEDGMENT
to Kirsten and Fred Thiam, who reviewed both the text and early sketches; to Ruth
Weinreb for her lightning fast translation help; and to everyone at Team Viking,
including especially that goddess among editors, Melanie Cecka.

VIKING
Published by Penguin Group
Penguin Young Readers Group, 345 Hudson Street, New York, New York 10014, U.S.A.

Penguin Books Ltd, Registered Offices: 80 Strand, London WC2R 0RL, England

First published in 2005 by Viking, a division of Penguin Young Readers Group

1 3 5 7 9 10 8 6 4 2

LIBRARY OF CONGRESS CATALOGING-IN-PUBLICATION DATA
Young, Amy.
Belinda in Paris / by Amy Young.
p. cm.
Summary: When Belinda's magnificently large ballet shoes get lost en route to Paris,
she must find another pair before her performance in the Paris Opera.
ISBN 0-670-03693-5 (hardcover)
[1. Foot—Fiction. 2. Size—Fiction. 3. Ballet dancers—Fiction. 4. Shoes—Fiction.
5. Paris (France)—Fiction. 6. France—Fiction.] I. Title.
PZ7.844Be 2005   [E]—dc22   2004001666

Manufactured in Mexico   Set in Mrs Eaves Roman and Weehah

You can find several real sites from Paris in this book: Page 3: The Eiffel Tower (background);
Page 6: view from the top of Notre Dame Cathedral; Pages 14-15: The Garden of the Tuileries,
Carrousel Arch, and the Louvre; Page 17: Sainte Chappelle; Pages 28-29: The Paris Opera